Marvel's
Captain America: Civil War

Based on the Screenplay by
Christopher Markus and Stephen McFeely

Produced by Kevin Feige, p.g.a.
Directed by Anthony and Joe Russ

Level 3

Retold by Coleen Degnan-Veness

Series Editors: Andy Hopkins and Jocelyn Potter

Pearson Education Limited

KAO Two

KAO Park, Harlow,

Essex, CM17 9NA, England

and Associated Companies throughout the world.

ISBN: 978-1-292-20591-5

This edition first published by Pearson Education Ltd 2018

5 7 9 10 8 6

The authors have asserted their moral rights in accordance
with the Copyright Designs and Patents Act 1988

Set in 9pt/14pt Xenois Slab Pro

SWTC/05

Published by Pearson Education Limited

For a complete list of the titles available in the Pearson English Readers series, visit
www.pearsonenglishreaders.com.
Alternatively, write to your local Pearson Education office or
to Pearson English Readers Marketing Department,
Pearson Education, KAO Two, KAO Park, Harlow, Essex, CM17 9NA

Contents

Who's Who?

Steve Rogers / Captain America

He fought for his country, then almost died in the ocean. After seventy years under the Arctic ice, he was saved. He then became one of the first Avengers. His weapon is his shield, made from a very strong metal from Wakanda.

Tony Stark / Iron Man

A very smart man, he makes a lot of money from his company, Stark Industries. While he was the prisoner of the Ten Rings, a terrorist organization, he built an armored suit. He used it to escape, added weapons to the suit, and became Iron Man.

James Buchanan ("Bucky") Barnes

As a child and young man he was a close friend of Steve Rogers. When he was caught by the terrorist group Hydra at the end of World War II, he was brainwashed. He became a Winter Soldier, a super-soldier, for them.

Prince T'Challa / Black Panther

He is a king's son from the African country of Wakanda. He fights in a cat suit with many different weapons or with none. He usually fights alone to protect his country. In this story, though, he wants to avenge a death.

Brock Rumlow / Crossbones

He is a great street fighter who worked for the terrorist group Hydra. He tried to kill Captain America for Hydra, and in the fight his face was very badly burned. He now works alone.

Thaddeus Ross

He was a top soldier, but is now the U.S. Secretary of State and works with other governments around the world. (Everett Ross works for him in the fight against terrorism, but isn't a relative.)

Team Iron Man

Natasha Romanoff / Black Widow is a spy and skillful fighter. Vision, a robot, can defend himself against powerful attacks, fly, walk through walls, and see everything. James ("Rhodey") Rhodes / War Machine has been Stark's close friend since they fought together for the American government. Black Panther is a mysterious fighter who usually fights alone to protect his country.

Team Captain America

Sam Wilson / Falcon wears a suit with wings and can fly very fast. Scott Lang / Ant-Man can become very small or very large. Wanda Maximoff / Scarlet Witch can move things with her mind, and can stop attacks, make explosions, and start fires with her fingers. Clint Barton / Hawkeye has no superpowers, but can shoot very well. James Buchanan ("Bucky") Barnes became a super-soldier for the terrorist group Hydra after after they brainwashed him.

Introduction

"We're failing ourselves if we don't act bravely. We must defend our actions," he said.

Captain America is speaking to the other Avengers. He doesn't believe that they should sign the Sokovia Accords. These are an international agreement giving governments power over the Avengers' actions. The agreement is needed—they are told—because people around the world are angry about the Avengers' deadly mistakes. After signing this new agreement, the Avengers will only be able to fight outside the United States with permission from an international organization.

Some of the Avengers don't like the idea of the agreement much, but decide to sign. Others think that it is a good idea. But Captain America believes that the Avengers need to be free. He thinks that no government can protect the world as well as super heroes.

When Iron Man agrees to sign, the Avengers break into two groups—Iron Man's against Captain America's—and the result is a terrible civil war. But it is not clear who their real enemy is. And it is not clear how this fight will end.

In the 2016 movie of Marvel's *Captain America: Civil War*, Chris Evans plays Captain America, Robert Downey Jr. is Iron Man, and Scarlett Johansson plays Black Widow. The movie earned more than $1.1 billion.

The story is about problems between super heroes who are also friends. These are real-life problems, of course. There is plenty of action to enjoy in this story. But readers will also think about the kind of world that they want to live in.

The Winter Soldier

1991

In Siberia, Karpov opened a small locked cupboard and took from it a small red book with a black star on the cover. Then he woke James Buchanan Barnes from a deep sleep. Barnes was taken to a secret room, moving more like a robot than a man. In that room was a brainwashing machine used in the past by the terrorist organization Hydra.

By 1991, after many fights against Captain America and the Avengers, Hydra was already destroyed and most of its soldiers were dead. But Karpov lived and he wanted to rebuild Hydra.

He tied Barnes to a chair and turned the brainwashing machine on. The machine's metal arms held Barnes's head and pushed.

"*Aaargh!*" screamed Barnes.

Karpov began reading a list of Russian words from the book. These words had the power to brainwash a man's mind. When he finished, Barnes broke out of the chair. He stood up straight.

"Good morning, soldier," Karpov said, now speaking in English.

"Ready for action," the Winter Soldier replied.

"I have a job for you. Nobody must know."

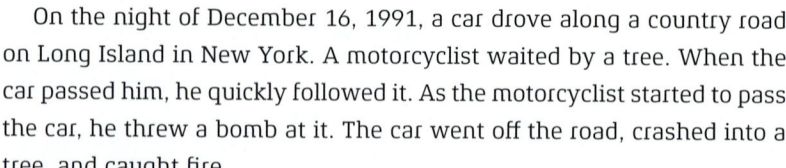

On the night of December 16, 1991, a car drove along a country road on Long Island in New York. A motorcyclist waited by a tree. When the car passed him, he quickly followed it. As the motorcyclist started to pass the car, he threw a bomb at it. The car went off the road, crashed into a tree, and caught fire.

The motorcyclist opened the back of the car. There he found five blue bags of chemicals.

Back in Siberia, Karpov looked at the bags of chemicals and said, "Well done, soldier." He needed these chemicals to brainwash more men.

Present Day

In Cleveland, Ohio, Karpov sat at a table in a small, dark apartment, eating his lunch. Suddenly, he heard a crash. Then there was a knock on his door.

Karpov didn't move.

"I drove into your car," a man shouted. "Can we talk about it? Or shall we call the police?"

"No, no police," said Karpov.

When he opened the door, a stranger hit him hard in the face. Karpov fell to the floor and the stranger tied him up. Then, using a large metal tool, the stranger broke a hole in the living room wall. There he found some papers and the small red book with a black star on the cover.

"Give me the report on December 16, 1991," the stranger said.

"Who are you?" Karpov asked, afraid for his life.

"My name is Zemo."

"What do you want?" asked Karpov.

"The report on December 16, 1991," Zemo repeated.

"Never!"

"I need this book," Zemo said. "Give me the information I want. Then I will not kill you."

"Never!" said Karpov—so Zemo killed him.

Making the World Safer

"What do you see?" asked Captain America, looking out the window of a hotel room in downtown Lagos, in Nigeria.

Wanda Maximoff was sitting in a coffee shop across the street and could hear him through her electronic ear piece.

"A quiet street ... police in front of the police station," she answered softly.

She looked down at the newspaper in front of her, at a photo of Brock Rumlow below the words "Weapons Sold to Terrorists."

In his last big fight for the terrorist organization Hydra, Rumlow was almost killed and suffered very serious burns to his face. After that, he wore a death mask and used the name Crossbones. He worked for himself and stole weapons around the world, often from police stations.

Captain America, in Lagos with Wanda, Natasha Romanoff, and Falcon, had information that Rumlow was planning to bomb the Lagos police station. The Avengers had a history with Rumlow and they had to stop him this time.

"Do you see that big vehicle over there?" Captain America asked.

"The red one? It's nice," Wanda answered.

Natasha sat down near Wanda in the coffee shop.

"It's also protected against bullets," her voice said in Wanda's ear piece. "That means *they* have guns."

"You guys know that I can move things with my mind, right?" said Wanda.

Wanda Maximoff's family was accidentally killed in Sokovia by an Avengers' bomb, made by Stark Industries. For years, Wanda planned to avenge her family's deaths by killing Tony Stark. But then she discovered that Tony Stark was Iron Man, one of her heroes. She changed her mind. She, too, wanted to help people in danger, so she joined the Avengers.

Falcon was in the area of the police station and coffee shop. Captain America noticed a truck that was very low on the ground. He spoke to Falcon through his ear piece.

"Sam, do you see that truck?" Captain America asked. "Search it!"

Falcon's drone flew out of the bag on his back and under the truck. The cameras on the drone showed him what was below it.

"The truck's weighed down with rocks and the driver has a weapon," Falcon told Captain America.

The four Avengers raced to stop the truck. They were too late. *CRASH!* It drove into the building across the street from the police station—a building where scientists worked on deadly chemical weapons. The driver jumped out and was joined—from two other trucks—by ten more men. They wore black suits with gas masks over their faces and carried guns. One of the men was Crossbones.

The men ran inside and threw cans of gas. Immediately, the building filled with thick black smoke. Guards had to run outside for air. Inside, people were coughing and falling to the floor.

Crossbones and his men started attacking the Avengers.

POW! Captain America easily protected himself from their bullets with his shield as he pushed a truck into one of them. *OOMPH!* He kicked another man into a wall. *ZAP!* Bullets from Falcon's wing suit shot and killed another.

"Five men dead," Falcon said to Captain America.

Crossbones's men continued shooting. With one hand, Scarlet Witch easily pushed their bullets away. She picked up one of the men and threw

With one hand, Scarlet Witch easily pushed their bullets away.

him against a wall. *BANG!* Falcon shot him dead.

"Rumlow's on the third floor," he shouted.

Captain America told Black Widow, "Do exactly as we practiced."

"What about the gas?" she asked.

"Get it out of there!" he told Scarlet Witch.

Crossbones and his men ran straight to the room with the deadly chemicals—chemical weapons that could kill millions of people. They found the bottle that they wanted inside a strong glass box. *CRASH!* Crossbones broke the glass and took the bottle.

With her powerful fingers, Scarlet Witch pulled the gas out of the building through the windows, and sent it up into the sky.

Falcon touched a small machine on his wrist and a bomb shot from the bag on his back. *BANG!* It killed another man.

Pulling off his gas mask, Crossbones walked out of the building. He looked up at the smoke.

"Captain America's here," he said to one of his men. Crossbones wanted his old enemy dead.

"Rumlow has a chemical weapon," Captain America told Black Widow. "We have to get it back!"

"I'm on my way!" she said.

She jumped on a motorcycle and sped after them. When she got close, she jumped from the motorcycle onto the roof of their truck. *THWACK! ZAP!* She fought each man as he tried to kill her. She kicked and hit hard. *BOOM!* Crossbones tried to kill her with a bomb. But she got away before it exploded.

Crossbones and four of his men jumped into their trucks. From the large gun on the roof of one, Crossbones shot at Captain America. *WHAM!* It hit him and Captain America flew off the building and onto his back.

"Falcon?" said Captain America, trying to get up.

"He's going north," Falcon replied.

Crossbones told his men, "Leave the truck!"

The men jumped out of the truck and ran through the busy streets. Falcon and Black Widow followed close behind. Around them, hundreds of people were running and screaming.

Crossbones kicked Captain America to the ground again.

"Here you are," he said angrily. "I've waited for this for a long time!"

Not far away, Black Widow came face to face with the man who had the chemical weapon now. They each pointed a gun at the other.

"Drop the gun," the man said to Black Widow, "or I'll drop this." He held up the bottle.

Suddenly, *BAMM!* Falcon's drone shot him and he dropped the bottle. Black Widow quickly caught it before it hit the ground.

She looked straight at Falcon's drone and said, "Thank you, Sam. I've got it."

Falcon received her message immediately. "Good," he answered.

Not far away, Crossbones pulled out his knife. Before he could push it into Captain America's neck, Captain America threw Crossbones hard against a wall. Crossbones fell to the ground. He pulled off his mask and Captain America saw the terrible burns on his face.

"Who's your buyer?" Captain America asked angrily.

"Your old friend, Bucky Barnes," replied Crossbones with a smile.

"What did you say?" Captain America asked, very surprised. Was Bucky really still alive?

Many years ago, Barnes was caught by a Russian scientist, and brainwashed. Rogers's old friend became a killing machine, working for the terrorist group Hydra. But that was long ago.

"He remembered you," said Crossbones. "He almost cried when he was

"Who's your buyer?" Captain America asked angrily. "Your old friend, Bucky Barnes," replied Crossbones with a smile.

talking about you. But then Hydra brainwashed him again. He told me to tell you this: 'We all have to die some time. It's my time.'" Crossbones looked into Captain America's eyes. "And it's your time now!'"

Crossbones reached for the bomb that was hidden inside his suit. But Scarlet Witch pointed her superpower fingers at him and Captain America quickly jumped out of the way. Crossbones's bomb exploded, sending him up into the air in a ball of fire.

Scarlet Witch's fingers held the explosion safely above the people on the ground, but the red ball grew bigger and bigger—and her powers were getting weaker. She couldn't hold onto the ball of fire. Suddenly, it hit the side of a large hotel, destroying it.

Scarlet Witch stood silently, watching the hotel burn, with tears in her eyes. "I tried—but I failed," she thought. How many people were dying up there?

"Oh, no …! We need firefighters and doctors on the south side of the building urgently!" Captain America shouted to Falcon.

Captain America saw the terrible burns on his face.

The Sokovia Accords

"Last month, when twenty-six people were killed in a Lagos hotel," the T.V. news reporter said, "eleven of them were visiting from the small, rich African country of Wakanda. They were there as friends, to help poor Nigerians."

In the Avengers' main office building in New York State, Steve Rogers and Wanda Maximoff watched the news report. They listened to King T'Chaka talk about the Wakandan people who lost their lives.

"Our people were killed in a foreign country by the illegal actions of criminals and by the people who promised to stop them," said the king. "The terrorists were criminals—but the Avengers were also working illegally."

The news reporter turned to his viewers. "Why should Wanda Maximoff, with her superpowers, be able to fight in Nigeria?" he agreed.

Rogers turned the T.V. off.

"I killed them," Wanda said sadly.

"That's not true," Rogers said. "I didn't see Crossbones's bomb until it was too late. People died because I didn't act quickly enough. We always try to save as many people as we can. Sometimes we can't save everybody. We have to live with that, or the next time we won't save anybody."

Suddenly, Vision walked through a wall and into the room.

"Vision, we've talked about this!" Wanda said. She really didn't like it when he came into a room through the wall.

"Sorry," Vision said. Then he turned to Rogers. "Secretary Ross wants to see you, and Mr. Stark, and all of the Avengers team, in his office."

"I'll be there in a minute," answered Rogers.

"I'll use the door," Vision said to Wanda as he left.

Rogers, Wanda, Natasha, Wilson, Stark, and James "Rhodey" Rhodes met in the office of Thaddeus Ross, the Secretary of State.

"People around the world know that for many years the Avengers have fought for us," said Secretary Ross. "You've protected us. You're heroes to a lot of people—but to some, you are not."

"What's *your* opinion?" asked Natasha.

"I think you can be described as dangerous," he answered slowly. "You're a group of people with special powers who go from the United States into other people's countries. You don't seem to think about ordinary people's lives. Many get hurt."

Secretary Ross turned on a video, showing Avengers' bombs destroying buildings in New York, Washington, D.C., Sokovia, Johannesburg, and Lagos.

"O.K., that's enough," Rogers said after a few minutes. The pictures were terrible and the Avengers hated them. Some of his friends were beginning to hate themselves for killing so many people.

"For the past four years, you haven't had to ask permission to fight the enemy in other countries," Secretary Ross said. "But after Lagos, world opinion has changed. There have been too many deaths. We're going to solve this problem with a new law, the Sokovia Accords. When this is signed, the Avengers won't be a private organization."

He gave a thick book to Natasha with the words "Sokovia Accords" on the cover. She passed it to the others.

"In three days' time, the United Nations* will meet in Vienna to agree on this," said Secretary Ross. "One hundred and seventeen countries are ready to sign it. Under this agreement, you will act *only* when the United Nations decides."

---

*United Nations: an international organization of 193 countries. They meet to try to solve the world's problems. The organization can then act on their agreements.

Rogers wasn't happy. "We started the Avengers to make the world a safer place," he said. "I feel that we've done that."

"Three days from now, the United Nations is going to meet in Vienna to sign this agreement. Talk about it," said Secretary Ross, and he walked to the door.

"And if you don't like our decision …?" asked Natasha.

"Then you must stop all your Avengers activities," answered Ross, and left.

The Avengers sat and discussed the agreement for more than an hour. Rogers didn't like the idea. Wilson agreed with Rogers. Rhodes thought it was a good idea. They could all work in a more organized way.

The Avengers sat and discussed the agreement for more than an hour.

Vision agreed with Rhodes. "Haven't you noticed?" he said. "As the number of Avengers has grown, there have been more—not fewer—possibly world-ending problems."

"You haven't said anything, Tony," Natasha said to Stark.

"I've made a lot of mistakes in my life," he answered. "I saw what my company's weapons were doing to people. So I stopped making them. People want to feel safe. I don't think we should keep people awake at night in fear. We should sign."

Stark could never forget the death of a young man, Charlie Spencer, in Sokovia. When Stark spoke at a college in the United States after the attack, Charlie Spencer's mother was there. She was very angry.

"Charlie went to Sokovia for the summer before he started college," she told Stark. "He was helping poor people—but you killed him."

Stark couldn't get her words out of his head—but Rogers had a different opinion.

"We're failing ourselves if we don't act bravely. We must defend our actions," he said. "If we sign this, we'll give up something very important. What will happen if the United Nations stops us helping people in danger?"

He looked at his team, his friends.

"Maybe Tony's right," said Natasha slowly. "We've made some very big mistakes. If we don't sign this now, they'll punish us later."

Rogers couldn't believe his ears. He looked at her, stood up, and left.

"I'm going to Vienna, and I'm going to sign the Sokovia Accords," Natasha told Rogers twenty-four hours later. The two of them were alone.

"Who's already signed?" Rogers asked.

"Tony, Rhodey, and Vision."

"Clint Barton?"

"He's decided to stop working for the Avengers," answered Natasha. "He wants to spend more time with his family."

"Wanda?" asked Rogers.

"Not yet," she answered. "Come with me to Vienna, Steve. We can do this together."

"I'm sorry. I can't," Rogers said.

Inside the United Nations building in Vienna, Natasha kept her eyes open for terrorists. It was the perfect place for an attack. A terrorist could kill a lot of presidents, princes, and kings with one bomb. King T'Chaka of Wakanda and his son, Prince T'Challa, were there, of course. They crossed the room to speak to her.

"The Avengers are sorry about the deaths of your people in Nigeria," Natasha said.

"Thank you," King T'Chaka replied. "And thank you for coming here today. It's not easy to give up power. But I'm sad that Captain America isn't here."

"Yes, I'm sad, too," Natasha agreed.

The room was silent. It was time for King T'Chaka's speech.

"I am grateful to those Avengers who joined us here today ..." he began.

As he spoke, his son looked out the window. He noticed a van in front of the building. Something about the van was wrong.

"Everyone, get down!" Prince T'Challa shouted.

KABOOM!

Windows exploded and bodies were thrown into the air. King T'Chaka was hit by a large piece of glass. His son ran to him, but it was too late; the king was dead. Prince T'Challa held his father in his arms and cried.

The Search for Bucky Barnes

"A bomb exploded at the United Nations building in Vienna today," said a T.V. news reporter. "It was hidden in a news van. More than seventy people were hurt and twelve are dead. One of them is Wakanda's King T'Chaka."

Rogers was watching the news report from a hotel room in the United States with his friend Sam Wilson.

The news reporter continued, "We now have a video of the bomber—James Buchanan Barnes, also known as the Winter Soldier. Hydra's most famous soldier has destroyed buildings and killed many politicians in terrorist attacks."

Rogers watched more carefully. The bomber in the video was his old friend, "Bucky" Barnes.

Outside the United Nations building in Vienna, Natasha found Prince T'Challa. He was looking at a picture of the Winter Soldier on his phone. She knew from the look in his eyes that he was planning to avenge his father's death.

"T'Challa, the police will catch Bucky Barnes," she said softly.

"*I* will catch him," said Prince T'Challa angrily, "and kill him."

He turned and walked away.

Natasha's phone rang. It was Rogers.

"Are you all right?" he asked.

"Yes, I got lucky," she replied. "Steve, I know how much Barnes means to you. I really do. But you should stay home. If you don't, you'll make this worse for all of us. You didn't sign the Sokovia Accords, and you can't work alone as Captain America. You'll be a criminal, and you'll be locked up. That's how things are now."

"I need to find Bucky before the police do," Rogers said. "I don't think he'll kill *me*."

He needed help. He found Wilson in a café.

"Did Natasha tell you to stay out of it?" Wilson asked. "Maybe she's right."

"Bucky needs my help," said Rogers.

"We have to think carefully about this. I don't like people shooting at you. They usually shoot at me, too," his friend said with a smile.

A woman walked in and stood next to Rogers. It was Sharon Carter, Rogers's old girlfriend. She worked for the U.S. government and arrived with a large envelope—secret information for Rogers about Barnes.

"You'll have to be quick if you want to find Bucky first," Sharon said. "We have orders. We'll shoot to kill."

Later that same day, in the streets of Romania's capital, Bucharest, Barnes saw his photo on the front page of a newspaper under the words "Winter Soldier Bombs United Nations Building in Vienna."

The newspaper seller looked at the photo, too, and then at Barnes. He left his newspapers and ran to the police station.

At the same time, Captain America was inside Barnes's Bucharest apartment. He looked around while, outside, Falcon watched for the German police. They were a special group that fought against terrorism.

With the permission of the Romanian government, they were searching for Barnes in Bucharest.

"Police cars are arriving from the south," Falcon reported.

Just then, Barnes arrived back at his apartment. He needed some clothes and then planned to leave the country.

He opened the door, and stopped.

Captain America turned and looked at him. "Do you know me?" he asked.

"You're Steve," answered Barnes slowly.

"Yeah. I can see that you're nervous," said Captain America.

"I wasn't in Vienna," Barnes told him. "I didn't bomb that building. I don't do that now."

Falcon reported urgently, "They're on the roof!"

"The police are coming. *They* think you did it," Captain America told Barnes. "They're not planning to take you alive. This doesn't have to end in a fight, Bucky."

"It always ends in a fight," replied Barnes.

"Five seconds!" called Falcon.

"You saved my life when you pulled me from the river in Washington, D.C." Captain America said. "Why did you do that?"

"Four seconds!" called Falcon.

"I don't know," Barnes replied.

"Yes, you do," said Captain America. "We were friends. And now *I'm* going to save *you*."

CRASH! A window broke as the police threw a bomb through it. Quickly, Captain American threw his shield on the bomb and covered the explosion. Just then, the door flew open. The police ran in, shooting. Captain America protected himself and Barnes from their bullets with his shield.

Barnes threw a bag out of the window and jumped out after it. On the ground, he picked up his bag with his passport, some weapons, and money inside it and ran.

Suddenly, *WHAM!*, a man in black landed on Barnes's back and fought like a wild cat.

Falcon watched from above.

"Who's that?" he asked Captain America, surprised.

"I'm going to find out," replied Captain America. He climbed out of the window and jumped off the roof into the street.

A police helicopter flew over the building and shot at Captain America, Barnes, and the man in black. Captain America noticed that the bullets didn't go through the stranger's suit.

"His suit is made of the same metal as my shield," Captain America realized. "Metal from Wakanda."

Barnes was running away fast now, but the man in black was close behind him. Captain America raced after them and Falcon followed. As the police helicopter got near, Falcon shot at it.

Barnes ran through the heavy traffic, jumping over cars. Captain America opened the door of a police vehicle and pulled the driver out. *ZOOM!* He sped toward Barnes. Then Barnes pushed a driver off his motorcycle. He, too, sped away.

Suddenly, the man in black jumped on the back of the motorcycle and pulled it over onto its side. He and Barnes fell into the road.

Suddenly, there were German police everywhere.

"Everyone, stop!" It was War Machine. "Don't shoot!" he told the police. "Don't kill them. Take them away." He turned to Captain America. "I don't want to do this, Captain, but you're a criminal now," War Machine said.

"I don't want to do this, Captain, but you're a criminal now," War Machine said.

The man in black pulled off his mask. It was Prince T'Challa!

The police put Captain America, Falcon, and the prince in one police vehicle and they locked Barnes inside a strong glass and metal box in another.

Falcon asked the prince, "Do you have special powers to fight crime?"

"Of course. I'm the Black Panther. There's a world outside of the Avengers," the prince replied seriously.

"I'm sorry about your father's death," Captain America said.

"Then why did you try to stop me killing Barnes?"

"Because you're going after the wrong man," Captain America told him.

"So why did he run?" asked Black Panther.

Captain America didn't have an answer.

Rogers, Wilson, and the prince were driven to Berlin and taken to the main offices of the German police. The U.S. Secretary of State's chief against terrorism, Everett Ross, was waiting for them there.

"What's going to happen to Barnes?" Rogers asked him.

"We'll interview him and give him tests. We need to learn more about his mind. Then we'll take him back to the United States," Ross replied.

Sharon Carter was standing next to Ross, not looking at Rogers. She didn't want her boss to know that she was giving Rogers information about his friend.

"Take their weapons," Ross ordered.

Captain America's shield, Black Panther's cat suit, and Falcon's wing suit were soon locked away.

"We won't put you in prison," said Ross. "We'll give you an office. Stay in it, please."

He took the three men to an office. There they were joined by Natasha and Stark.

"You've made things worse for yourself," Natasha said to Rogers.

"Bucky's still alive … so things aren't worse," he replied.

Stark was on the phone to the United States Secretary of State,

Thaddeus Ross.

"No, the Avengers didn't have permission to attack anyone in Romania," he said. "Yes, their action was illegal and we *will* punish them."

He felt uncomfortable. He knew that Rogers and Wilson could hear his side of the conversation. He ended the call quickly.

"Are they going to keep my shield?" Rogers asked Stark.

"It belongs to the United States government now," answered Natasha. "Your wings, too," she said to Wilson.

"Great," said Wilson.

"It's better than going to prison," said Natasha.

Later that day, when Stark was alone with Rogers in the office, he said, "We need you, Steve. If you sign the Sokovia Accords, Bucky will go to an American hospital and not to a Wakandan prison."

Rogers looked at Stark's pen on the desk in front of him.

"I don't know," he said thoughtfully.

"When things are calmer, perhaps we can make some changes to the agreement," Stark said. Rogers picked up the pen.

"We can get you and Wanda back into the Avengers ..."

"Wanda?" asked Rogers. "Is she O.K.?"

"She's in a safe place," said Stark. "Vision is looking after her."

"What?" Rogers said. "*What* safe place?"

"She's protected there ..." said Stark.

"Is she in a prison? That's *not* protecting her," said Rogers angrily.

"It's not a prison, but she can't leave," Stark explained. "She's not American, Steve, and she has dangerous superpowers. The American government doesn't want her out on the streets."

Rogers put the pen down without signing. He walked out.

Zemo's Plan

"Hello, Mr. Barnes. I was sent here by the United Nations to interview you," said the doctor.

In the Berlin police station, Everett Ross, Stark, Rogers, Natasha, and Sharon Carter could hear and see the interview on the office computers. Barnes and his interviewer were in another, safer part of the building.

Rogers looked at the photo of Barnes on his phone.

"I don't think that Barnes *was* the bomber," he said. "So why was his photo sent around the world? Who sent it?"

"Maybe someone wanted us to find him?" Sharon suggested.

"We searched for the guy for two years and couldn't find him," Wilson said.

"Yes, and then the United Nations building was bombed," said Rogers thoughtfully. "Everyone started looking …"

"Yes, and as a result we found him," Sharon agreed.

They looked hard at the doctor interviewing Barnes. They couldn't know that Barnes's interviewer wasn't, in fact, a doctor.

The real doctor was dead in his Berlin hotel room. The man in front of Barnes was Zemo, and he had a plan.

"So, Bucky, a lot of things have happened to you," Zemo said quietly.

"Tell me about them."

"I don't want to talk about them," said Barnes from inside the glass and metal box.

"It's O.K., Bucky. We only have to talk about one …"

Just then, Zemo got a message on his phone: "Job done."

KABOOM! A bomb exploded next to a power station in another part of the city, turning off the electricity across Berlin. Now Rogers and the others couldn't see or hear the interview on their computers.

Zemo quickly began his real work on Barnes. He opened the red book with a black star on the cover and started reading the Russian words from it in a slow, quiet voice. With these words, he was able to brainwash Barnes.

As he read, he walked closer and closer toward Barnes. Barnes held his head, screaming in terrible pain.

Bucky Barnes, now the Winter Soldier, broke out of the box.

"Soldier?" said Zemo.

"Ready for action," replied the Winter Soldier, in a robotic voice.

"Report: December 16, 1991," Zemo ordered.

"So, Bucky, a lot of things have happened to you," Zemo said quietly. "Tell me about them."

When the computers went off in Ross's office, everyone hurried out. Rogers and Wilson arrived outside the interview room. There they found bodies everywhere. Zemo was on the floor, but still alive.

"Help, help me," he said.

"Get up," said Rogers, pulling him to his feet. He pushed Zemo against the wall. "Who are you? What do you want?"

"I want to see some very powerful people fall," he answered, looking Rogers straight in the eye.

Which powerful people? Rogers knew that Barnes was the Winter Soldier again. They had to stop him.

But the Winter Soldier found *them*. THWACK! POW! After pushing Rogers down the stairs, he ran away. Wilson ran after him. Zemo disappeared.

In his dark office, Everett Ross spoke urgently on his phone: "Get everyone out of the building. Get gunships in the air!"

The Winter Soldier was a crazy, robotic fighter. Sharon Carter and Natasha joined the fight against him. *WHAM!* The Winter Soldier threw them to the ground. He jumped out of a window. Prince T'Challa jumped on him but the Winter Soldier got away.

The Winter Soldier ran up onto the roof of the police station and jumped into a helicopter. As the helicopter started to go up, Rogers ran toward it. He jumped up and, with his super-strong arms, pulled it back down. The helicopter crashed onto the roof and almost onto Rogers. Then it fell off the roof and into the river below. *CRASH!* Both men fell with it.

Rogers's head came up first. He looked around, and pulled Barnes out of the river. His old friend's eyes were closed, but he was alive. Rogers and Wilson took him to an empty building.

Some time later, Barnes woke up. "Steve?" he said.

"Which Bucky am I talking to?" asked Rogers.

"What did I do?" Barnes asked. He looked tired.

"Enough."

"Hydra put all that stuff in me and it's still there," said Barnes. "He only had to say those words and I became the Winter Soldier again."

"Who was he—your interviewer?" asked Rogers. "People died. The bombing … The man did that to get ten minutes with you. Why?"

"I don't know," Barnes replied. "He wanted to know about Siberia and where I was kept there."

"Why did he need to know that?" asked Rogers.

"Maybe because … I'm not the only Winter Soldier," Barnes replied sadly. "But he also wanted to know what happened on a night in 1991 … December 16." Rogers looked at him and Barnes continued. "After brainwashing me, Hydra sent me out that night on a motorcycle. They told me to steal some chemicals—chemicals for more brainwashing—from Howard Stark, the owner of Stark Industries." Rogers knew that he was talking about Tony Stark's father.

"I drove up next to his car and threw a small bomb into it. It crashed into a tree and the man and woman inside the car were badly hurt. I killed them. Then I opened the back of the car and found five bags of chemicals. I took them to Siberia, to Hydra. Those were my orders, and I followed them."

"So that was how Tony Stark's parents were killed," Rogers thought sadly.

"When Hydra put these chemicals into our bodies, we became Winter Soldiers—Hydra's special Death Team," Barnes said. "Together, we killed more people than anyone in Hydra's history."

"So they all became like you?"

"Worse."

"That 'doctor'—your interviewer? Will he have power over them, too, when he finds them?" Rogers asked.

"Yes," said Barnes.

"He wants to see some very powerful people fall, he said," Rogers told Barnes. "I'm not sure what he means."

"The Winter Soldiers can destroy a country in one night," said Barnes.

Wilson was listening. "Before the Sokovia Accords, it was easy for us to attack our enemies," he said. "But who's going to help us now?"

"If we call Tony …" Rogers began.

"He won't believe us," Wilson said. "And he'll have to ask the countries that signed the Sokovia Accords. They may not want him to help us."

"We have to do it alone," Rogers answered.

"Maybe not," said Wilson slowly. "I know a guy."

6

Iron Man Meets Spider-Man

"And you have no idea where Barnes, Rogers, and Wilson are?" Secretary of State Ross asked Stark.

"We'll find them. The German police are searching. They'll get information and we'll act on it."

"You don't understand, Stark," said Secretary Ross. "It's not your job now to act on it. I'm putting a special team on this. More people have died. Their lives matter!"

"You can't do this with boys and bullets. We'll find them," Stark said. "Give us seventy-two hours."

"I'll give you thirty-six. Get Barnes!" Secretary Ross ordered. "Get Rogers and Wilson, too!"

"Yes, sir. Thank you, sir," said Stark.

"We don't have enough people for this," Natasha said.

Stark agreed—they needed help.

The next day, Stark went to Queens, New York, to talk to Peter Parker. Peter was a high school student, and he lived with his aunt.

When he saw Tony Stark—Iron Man!—talking to his Aunt May in the living room, he was really surprised. She had no idea who their visitor was. Peter was sure of that.

Stark didn't want her to know the real reason for his visit. He told her about money that Peter could get from Stark Industries for his studies.

"Can I have five minutes alone with Peter?" he asked Aunt May finally.

"Sure," she answered.

Stark and Peter went into the boy's bedroom.

Stark took out his phone and showed Peter a video of Spider-Man. "That's you, right?" he asked.

"No," Peter answered. His other life was a secret one. "What do you mean?"

"I know it's you. You have unusual skills," Stark said as he closed his phone.

"It's not real. That video's done on a computer," Peter said nervously.

Stark noticed a small door above Peter's bed and opened it. A red and black Spider-Man suit and a metal can dropped down.

"Who knows that you're Spider-Man? Anybody?" asked Stark.

Peter shook his head. "Nobody," he replied.

"You know what's really great, in my opinion?" Stark said. "This webbing. Who made it?"

He threw the can of webbing to Peter.

"*I* did," answered Peter.

"And how do you climb walls?"

Before Peter could answer, Stark put Peter's Spider-Man glasses on. "Can you see with these?" he asked.

"Yes," said Peter and he took his glasses away from Stark.

"You need a new suit, more modern equipment. That's why I'm here," Stark told him. "Why do you do this?"

"I've been me all my life," answered Peter, "but I've had these superpowers for six months. Now I'm different. I have skills. And when someone does something wrong, I have to act."

Stark looked Peter straight in the eye. "So you want to look after the little guy and help him. You want to make the world a better place, right?" he asked.

"Yes, that's right," said Peter.

Stark sat down next to Peter. "Have you got a passport?" he asked.

"No," answered Peter.

"Have you ever been to Germany?" asked Stark.

"No," Peter replied.

"Oh, you'll love it!"

"I can't go to Germany!" said Peter. He looked surprised and worried.

"Why?"

"I ... I've got homework."

"I don't believe you said that," Stark laughed. Spider-Man's excuse was his homework!

"I'm serious! I can't just leave school!" said Peter nervously.

"I can tell your aunt that I'm taking you on a little trip," Stark said.

He walked to the door, but suddenly—*ZAPPP!*—Peter shot his special webbing over Stark's hand. Stark couldn't move.

"*Don't* tell Aunt May that I'm Spider-Man," said Peter seriously. "She doesn't know anything."

"All right." Stark smiled. "Now get me out of this."

Captain America's Team

There was a loud noise outside.

"What was that?" Wanda asked. She stood up and looked out the window.

"Stay here," said Vision.

He went outside to see.

Suddenly, Wanda knew that there was someone behind her. She sent a large kitchen knife flying toward his head. Then she turned and looked. It was Hawkeye.

"Oh!" she said. "What are *you* doing here?"

"Come with me, Wanda. Steve needs our help," said Hawkeye.

He took her hand and quickly walked toward the door.

Vision returned and looked angrily at Hawkeye. "Clint Barton, what are you doing here?"

Without a word, Hawkeye shot Vision. Then he kicked him, but his foot went straight through Vision's body.

"Clint, you can't stop me," said Vision calmly. He had his arm around Hawkeye's neck.

"I know I can't," said Hawkeye, trying hard to speak. Then, looking at Wanda, he said, "But *she* can."

"Vision, that's enough," said Wanda—and then she became Scarlet

Witch. She held up both hands and fired a shot from her fingers at Vision. "I'm leaving," she said, turning to go.

"You can't," Vision replied. He had to keep her there for her own protection. That was his promise to Tony Stark.

CRASH! Scarlet Witch sent Vision through the floor and deep down into the ground below. She and Hawkeye quickly left.

Rogers parked his car on the street and got out. Wilson and Barnes stayed inside. Another car drove up and stopped. Sharon Carter got out and opened the back so Rogers could look inside. There was his shield and Falcon's suit.

"Thank you, Sharon," he said gratefully.

She looked into his eyes and he looked into hers. They kissed.

They spoke for only a minute or two and then Sharon had to leave. Rogers turned and saw Wilson and Barnes smiling at him. He smiled, too.

He drove to the parking lot at Berlin airport and met Barton and Wanda. They were getting out of a white van.

"Thank you for coming," Rogers said to them. "Is our new guy here?"

"He's here and ready to go," said Barton, opening the back door of their van.

They spoke for only a minute or two and then Sharon had to leave.

A sleepy man got out and walked over to Rogers. They shook hands.

"Captain America!" said Scott Lang. He was Sam Wilson's friend. Wilson thought that he could help Captain America.

"Mr. Lang," said Rogers.

"I know you know a lot of skilled people," Lang said. "Thanks for thinking of me."

"We're going to do something illegal," Rogers told him. "If you join us, the police will be after you."

"Well, that's nothing new," said Lang.

"We have to go," Barnes said urgently.

"We have a helicopter ready," Barton said.

A loud voice came over the airport speakers. "Everyone, leave the airport!" the voice said in German.

"Stark's here," Rogers said to the others. "Put on your suits!"

Captain America ran toward the Avengers' helicopter. Immediately, it was attacked from above and he stopped. Down from the sky flew Iron Man and War Machine.

Iron Man pulled off his mask.

"Listen, Tony," Captain America told him. "The bomb in Vienna *wasn't* Bucky's work. It was the work of that man who interviewed him."

Suddenly, Black Panther was at his side. "Hello, Captain America," he said.

"Hello, King T'Challa," said Captain America. Since his father's death, the prince was the king of Wakanda.

"Ross gave me thirty-six hours to bring you in, Steve," said Iron Man. "And that was twenty-four hours ago." He was nervous and worried.

"You're going after the wrong guy. Barnes didn't do it," Captain America told him again.

"Your old friend killed people yesterday," Iron Man said angrily.

"And there are five more super-soldiers just like him," said Captain America. "That 'doctor' mustn't find them first, Tony. He really mustn't."

"Steve, you know what's going to happen. Do you really want to fight your way out of this?" Natasha asked him. "Avengers are going to fight Avengers. It will be a civil war!"

Avengers Attack Avengers

"I can't wait," Iron Man said. "Now!" he shouted.

WHOOSH! Spider-Man came out of the sky at great speed over Captain America's head. He shot at Captain America's shield with his special webbing—*THWACK!*—and easily pulled the shield away from him. This was Captain America's introduction to Spider-Man.

"Nice job, kid," Iron Man told him.

"Thanks," Spider-Man replied happily. "In my new suit, I couldn't stop as quickly as I usually do. But it's a perfect suit, Mr. Stark! Thank you."

"We don't talk while we're fighting," Iron Man told him.

"Hello, Captain America. I'm Spider-Man."

"That's enough. You can speak later," Iron Man told Spider-Man, in a fatherly voice. Then he turned and said, "Steve, you're being stupid! You've brought Clint Barton back into your team and taken Wanda from a safe place. I'm trying to stop you because I don't want you to start a civil war. Avengers shouldn't fight Avengers!"

"*You* started it when you signed the Sokovia Accords," Captain America told him.

"You're going to give Barnes to us and then you're going to come with us. You'll do that because it's *us*!" Iron Man told his friend.

Natasha listened and watched. She was very worried.

"We've found a plane that we can use," said Falcon's voice in Captain America's ear piece. His drone was sending a video of planes in a large airport building to Falcon's glasses.

War Machine, Black Panther, Black Widow, Vision, and Spider-Man were all ready to fight with Iron Man. On the other side, with Captain America, were Barnes, Falcon, Hawkeye, Scarlet Witch, and Ant-Man. They really didn't want to fight their friends, but they had to.

"All right, Lang!" said Captain America.

WHAM! Ant-Man became very, very small and attacked Spider-Man.

Spider-Man ... shot at Captain America's shield with his special webbing—
***THWACK!*—and easily pulled the shield away from him.**

"I'm going to get Wanda," said Iron Man. "Rhodey, you take Captain America."

"Barnes and Falcon are inside the airport," said Iron Man.

"Barnes is mine!" shouted Black Panther. He ran to find him.

"Mr. Stark, what do you want *me* to do?" asked Spider-Man.

"We discussed this! Tie them in webbing!" said Iron Man.

Spider-Man jumped up onto the roof, watched, and waited.

KER-BAM! Captain America threw his shield at Black Panther, and Black Panther fell to the ground. Immediately, he got back on his feet and the two fought again.

"I really don't want to hurt you," Ant-Man said to Black Widow. She didn't stop to answer. She attacked and he fought back.

Spider-Man jumped down from the roof and into the airport, and kicked Falcon to the floor.

POW! Barnes attacked Spider-Man.

Iron Man dropped bombs in front of Scarlet Witch and Hawkeye to stop them.

"What are you doing here?" Iron Man asked Hawkeye.

"Life at home was boring," Hawkeye answered.

Suddenly, the cars on the top floor of the parking lot came crashing down. Scarlet Witch was pulling them down with her superpowers. *CRASH!* Three cars fell on top of Iron Man.

Falcon flew through the airport, attacking Spider-Man. Spider-Man

was attacking Barnes.

Spider-Man locked Falcon's hands with his webbing.

"What are your wings made from?" he asked with interest.

Falcon looked at the webbing on his hands. "Is this stuff coming out of you?" he asked, surprised.

Spider-Man started to explain the science of his webbing, but Falcon stopped him.

"I don't know if you've been in a fight before," he said impatiently. "There's usually less talking."

"All right, sorry," said Spider-Man. "My mistake."

WHAM! He kicked Falcon and Barnes through some glass and onto the floor and locked their arms in his webbing.

"I have to do a good job for Mr. Stark today … so I'm really sorry, you guys," he said.

Captain America and his team were now running toward their plane. Suddenly, Vision arrived from high in the sky and spoke. They stopped and looked up at him.

"Captain America, you think that you are doing the right thing. But for everyone's good, you must give up now," he said.

Iron Man's team flew down and stood in front of Captain America's team.

"What do we do now, Captain?" Falcon asked quietly.

Captain America looked hard at Iron Man and his team. "We fight," he replied.

Iron Man's team flew down and stood in front of Captain America's team.

The Civil War

"They're not stopping," said Spider-Man.

"*We're* not stopping either," Iron Man replied.

Captain America's team raced across the airfield toward Iron Man's team; Iron Man's team were racing toward them, too. Everyone was prepared to fight this civil war to the end.

KAPOW! Iron Man hit Captain America, Black Panther attacked Barnes, and Hawkeye threw Black Widow to the ground.

"We're still friends, right?" Black Widow said, looking up at Hawkeye.

"We won't be friends if you hit me really hard," Hawkeye replied, smiling.

ZAP! Black Widow kicked him really hard, and he fell onto his back. Scarlet Witch saw them and sent Black Widow flying against a wall.

Black Panther had Barnes's neck in his hands. He was trying to kill him.

"I didn't kill your father," Barnes told him.

"Then why did you run?" Black Panther asked angrily.

Before Barnes could answer, Black Panther hit him: *WHAM! BANG!* Wanda came quickly to help Barnes. Black Panther was sent high up in the air and across the airfield at great speed until he crashed into a building.

Captain America threw his shield at Spider-Man, just missing him. It circled and returned to Captain America.

"That shield is no ordinary shield!" said Spider-Man.

"Listen, kid. There's a lot that you don't understand," said Captain America.

Spider-Man threw his webbing around Captain America's legs and pulled him toward him. Captain America crashed into him and his shield flew across the airfield. Captain America got up and ran after it, but Spider-Man's webbing locked his hands. Captain America's powers were too great and he threw Spider-Man up in the air. Now Spider-Man was on top of the walkway from a plane to the airport building.

"What has Stark told you about me?" asked Captain America.

"He says that you're wrong … But you think you're right," answered Spider-Man. "And that makes you dangerous."

KAPOW! Captain America threw his shield at the walkway. Spider-Man fell and the walkway crashed down on top of him. He held it up with his hands above his head.

"You've got heart, kid. Where are you from?" asked Captain America. He was beginning to like this young man with unusual superpowers.

"New York—Queens," Spider-Man answered, with difficulty. The walkway was very heavy. Could he hold it?

Captain America smiled and said, "I'm from Brooklyn."

While they were talking, Ant-Man, now very small, climbed inside Iron Man's suit and turned off the power to his weapons.

"Oh, no … what's happening?" Iron Man said to himself.

"We have to go," Barnes told Captain America. "That guy's probably in Siberia by now." He urgently wanted to find the unknown "doctor" who interviewed him.

Falcon was flying overhead, listening to their conversation.

"We have to stop the flyers, Sam," said Captain America. "I'll fight Vision. You get to the plane."

"No, you get to the plane," Falcon said. "You and Barnes. The rest of us aren't getting out of here. This isn't the real fight, Steve."

"All right, Sam. What's your idea?" Captain America asked.

Listening, Hawkeye said, "If some of us are going to win this fight, some of us are going to have to lose it."

"We need to stop their fighting. We need a big idea," said Falcon.

"I've got something big," said Ant-Man. "But I can't hold it for very long … When I say 'GO!' run fast. And if I break in half, don't come back for me."

"Are you sure about this, Scott?" asked Captain America.

"I do it all the time!" he answered fearlessly. "Well, that's not true—I did it once."

Suddenly, he changed himself into a very large Ant-Man, very much larger than everyone there. He took War Machine by the leg and held him up above his head. War Machine looked as small as a child's toy.

"GO!" shouted Ant-Man.

"I like his big idea," said Captain America.

"Great job, Ant-Man!" shouted Falcon, smiling.

When Iron Man saw the super-large Ant-Man holding War Machine up in the air, he shouted, "Give me back my Rhodey!"

Ant-Man threw War Machine across the sky like a child's paper airplane.

Speaking to his team, Iron Man asked, "Does anyone have any surprising skills that they never told me about? Now is the time to tell me." He really needed more help.

WHACK! Suddenly, Falcon sent his drone crashing into Iron Man's head.

Black Panther was trying to get around Ant-Man's large legs.

"Do you want to reach those guys over there?" Ant-Man asked him. "If you do, you have to go through me."

He opened his legs and almost killed Black Panther under one of his very large feet.

Spider-Man attacked Ant-Man, locking his legs in webbing. Then War Machine and Spider-Man attacked Ant-Man.

THWACK! Hawkeye shot his weapon at Black Panther.

"We haven't met yet. I'm Clint," Hawkeye said, introducing himself.

"I'm not interested," Black Panther told him.

War Machine and Ant-Man were fighting hard. Ant-Man was destroying cars and planes with every step.

Suddenly, Vision flew toward Ant-Man—and flew straight through his body!

"Something just flew *into* me!" screamed Ant-Man unhappily.

Vision destroyed part of the airport building and it came crashing down in front of Captain America and Barnes. They had to stop running, but were soon able to continue.

Black Widow stopped in front of Captain America. They stood face to face.

"You're not going to stop?" asked Black Widow.

"You know I can't," Captain America answered.

"This is going to get me into a lot of trouble," she said, "but I'm going to help you."

She shot at Black Panther before he could attack Captain America and Barnes.

"Go!" she told Captain America.

While Captain America and Barnes escaped, Spider-Man threw webbing around Ant-Man's legs. *POW!* Ant-Man hit Spider-Man hard and Spider-Man fell. Ant-Man fell on his back, destroying the plane behind him. With his superpowers, he made himself man-sized again.

He felt weak. He needed sugar. "Does anyone have an orange?" he asked.

Spider-Man was on the ground. Iron Man flew down to him.

"Kid, are you all right?" he asked, going down on his knees next to him.

Spider-Man was tired and weak. "Hi, man," he said in a quiet voice.

"Your work here is finished. You did a great job. You're going home," said Iron Man.

"No, no … I can't stop!" Spider-Man said.

"I'll call Aunt May …" said Iron Man.

"No, I'm not ready to leave," said Spider-Man. But when he tried to get up, he fell back onto the ground. "O.K.," he said quietly, "I'm finished."

10

Secrets in Siberia

"I wanted to help you find Barnes. I didn't want to help you *catch* him," Black Widow told Black Panther. "There's a difference."

After getting into the plane, Captain America and Barnes were finally on their way to Siberia. Black Panther watched them go.

Vision found Scarlet Witch sitting on the ground.

"I'm sorry," he said.

"I'm sorry, too," she replied. She understood why Vision tried to stop her going with Barton. And she felt bad about using her superpowers on him.

"I told you … Everything is being destroyed," Vision said. He looked into her eyes and felt a strange, warm feeling in his heart.

Falcon and Hawkeye flew behind Captain America and Barnes. Iron Man and War Machine were not far behind, shooting at them. Falcon looked back and shot at War Machine; War Machine dropped out of the sky onto a field. He was very badly hurt.

"RHODEY!" shouted Iron Man.

Iron Man flew down, landing on his knees next to his friend. War Machine's eyes were closed and he didn't move. Iron Man took War Machine's mask off, and saw blood on his face.

Next came Falcon. "I'm sorry," he said to Iron Man. He knew that Stark loved Rhodes like a brother.

ZAP! Iron Man shot Falcon away from him. Quickly, he called for help.

Vision flew down onto the field in front of Iron Man and looked down at the dying War Machine. He felt very bad about not protecting his team better.

Iron Man flew down, landing on his knees next to his friend. War Machine's eyes were closed and he didn't move.

Later, in the hospital, while the doctors were doing tests on Rhodes, Stark and Vision waited for the results.

"How did this happen?" Stark asked Vision angrily.

"I was looking the other way for a few seconds, talking to Wanda," answered Vision, deeply sorry. "I made a mistake."

"I didn't think that was possible," Stark said coldly.

"I didn't either," replied Vision, with a heavy heart.

When Natasha arrived, Stark looked at her angrily.

"Rhodey will probably never walk again," he said.

"Steve's not going to stop," Natasha said. "If *you* don't stop either, things will become worse."

"Why did you help Steve and Bucky get on that plane?" Stark asked.

"I realized that we were on the wrong side," Natasha told him.

"Ross knows what you did," said Stark. "They'll come for you."

"*I'm* not the one who needs to look over my shoulder," said Natasha, and she walked away.

Suddenly, a message from Stark's electronic secretary arrived on the machine on his wrist. It showed a photo, sent by the Berlin police. There was no time to lose! Stark left the hospital and jumped inside the Avengers' helicopter. There, he was sent more photos. One was of a Dr. Theo Broussard. He was the real doctor sent by the United Nations for Barnes's interview. Another photo was of the man who took the doctor's place. His name, Stark learned for the first time, was Helmut Zemo. He was the Sokovian chief of a secret group of killers.

"What happened to the real Dr. Broussard?" Stark asked his electronic secretary.

"He was found dead in a Berlin hotel room," she answered. "A mask of a face very similar to Barnes's face was found there, too."

"Send this photo of Zemo to Secretary Ross!" said Stark. "Rogers is following him. I need to find them—now!"

"Yes, boss," his secretary answered.

While Stark was learning about Zemo, Zemo was breaking into Hydra's secret hiding place in Siberia. With a light in his hand, he found a box with the date December 16, 1991, on it. Inside were old video tapes. He looked at them with interest. Then he walked into a larger room. There were the bodies of the other Winter Soldiers. They were either dead or in a deep sleep.

In the middle of the ocean, Stark brought down the helicopter on the roof of the United Nations' secret prison. Leaving the helicopter, he went to the door. There, he was met by Secretary Ross. Ross took him inside, past guards with guns.

Stark saw Wanda sitting behind bars in a small part of the room. She looked up at him but said nothing. He walked past her and into another room. He knew that Ross was watching him on video. There were cameras everywhere.

When Clint Barton saw Stark, he shouted from behind bars to his friends. "The great man is here! He knows what's best for you!"

"O.K., Barton, I had no idea that they wanted to put you here," said Stark quietly.

In the middle of the ocean, Stark brought down the helicopter on the roof of the United Nations' secret prison.

"Well, you knew that they wanted to put us *somewhere*, Tony," Barton replied angrily.

"This is a place for crazy people, not for …" said Stark, looking around.

"Criminals," Barton said, finishing Stark's sentence. "I think that's the word. That didn't mean me, or Sam, or Wanda ever before, but here we are."

"Because you broke the law," said Stark. "I didn't ask you to. You read the Sokovia Accords and you broke the agreement. You're a grown man. You have a wife and kid. I don't understand … Why didn't you think about *them* before you chose the wrong side?" He walked away.

Hitting the bars, Barton shouted, "You should watch your back, everyone! He'll probably break it!"

When Stark got to Wilson, he stopped. Wilson didn't look at him, but he asked, "How's Rhodey?"

"The doctors are flying him to a specialist hospital tomorrow," said Stark. "We hope that they'll be able to help him there. I want to know where Steve and Bucky are, Sam." He touched his electronic wrist machine. "I've turned off Ross's cameras and recording equipment," he said, looking at Wilson. "We have about thirty seconds. Then they'll realize that the problem's not with their equipment."

"What's happening?" Secretary Ross shouted at the man in front of the computers. "Get these machines working again!"

Stark showed Wilson the photo of the dead Dr. Broussard.

"*This* man was sent by the United Nations to interview Bucky Barnes. Sam, I made a mistake. I was wrong."

"That's a first," said Wilson. "You've never said that before!"

"Steve needs all the help that he can get," Stark continued.

"I'll tell you where they are," Wilson said, looking Stark in the eye. "But you have to go alone, and as a friend."

"Easy," replied Stark.

"Siberia," Wilson said, and told him exactly where.

Stark quickly walked back to the helicopter.

Secretary Ross stopped him. "Did he tell you anything about Rogers?" he asked.

"No," Stark replied.

High in the night sky, he changed into Iron Man and flew out of the helicopter.

Barnes asked, "What's going to happen to your friends, Steve? Maybe it wasn't a good idea to help me."

Rogers answered, "All those crimes … they weren't you. You didn't *choose* to do those things."

"I know, but I did them," said Barnes quietly.

They arrived at Hydra's secret hiding place in Siberia.

"My interviewer is probably already here," Barnes said.

"Then maybe he's already woken up the other Winter Soldiers," Rogers said seriously.

He quickly changed into Captain America. He held his shield in front of himself for protection while Barnes held a large gun. They walked slowly inside, looking everywhere.

Suddenly—*THUD!*—a heavy door opened behind them. They turned around fast, ready to attack.

Iron Man took off his mask and walked toward Captain America. Captain America walked toward him. He still had his shield in front of him.

"You seem defensive," Iron Man said.

"Yes, it's been a long day," answered Captain America.

"Don't worry, soldier," Iron Man said. "I'm not here to catch you."

"So why *are* you here?" asked Captain America.

"It seems that maybe your story wasn't crazy," Iron Man replied. "But Secretary Ross doesn't know that I'm here. I'd like to keep it that way."

"It's good to see you, Tony," said Captain America.

"It's good to see you, too, Captain." Turning to Barnes, Iron Man said, "You can put down your gun. We've stopped fighting."

Iron Man put his mask on again. Then he, Captain America, and

Barnes walked farther inside, into a large, dark room. There were glass cases filled with light and smoke.

A voice said, "The other Winter Soldiers all died in their sleep." It was the voice of Helmut Zemo. They walked closer to the cases and saw dead men.

"Did you really think that I wanted more Winter Soldiers?" Zemo asked. "I'm grateful to them, though. *They* brought you here."

"You killed people in Vienna because you wanted to bring us here?" Captain America asked Zemo.

"Yes, I made my plan more than a year ago," Zemo said. He stepped out of the darkness and looked Captain America straight in the eye. "I studied you. I followed you."

"I can tell from your voice that you're Sokovian," said Captain America. "Are you avenging your country?"

"Sokovia was a failed state a long time before you completely destroyed it. No, I'm here because I made a promise."

"You lost someone? Someone died in the attacks?" Captain America asked.

"I lost *everyone*," said Zemo. "And *you* will lose people, too."

Zemo turned on a computer and stepped away. Captain America looked at the computer. He saw the date December 16, 1991.

Standing behind him, Zemo said, "Destroyed by its enemies, a powerful group can come back to life. But if that powerful group destroys itself in a civil war, it's finished."

Captain America looked over his shoulder at Zemo, worried.

Iron Man walked to the computer and took off his mask. He looked at the date on an old video of a country road.

"I know that road," Iron Man said. "What is this?" he asked nervously.

The video started to play. He saw … his parents' car! A man on a motorcycle drove up to the car and threw a small bomb through the window. The car crashed into a tree and the driver fell out. The motorcyclist got off and pulled Howard Stark's head up by his white hair. Mr. Stark looked at the man and said weakly, "Mr. Barnes?" Iron Man looked hard at Barnes.

As Barnes watched the video, painful memories of his life as a Winter Soldier came back to him. They heard Mrs. Stark's voice calling for her husband. The Winter Soldier pulled Mr. Stark back into the car. Then he went to the other side of the car, put his hand around Stark's mother's neck, and killed her.

Iron Man turned to Captain America and asked angrily, "*Did you know?*"

"I didn't know it was him," said Captain America.

"Don't try to save your friend. Did you know?" Iron Man asked again, his voice shaking.

As Barnes watched the video, painful memories of his life as a Winter Soldier came back to him.

"Yes," answered Captain America quietly.

POW! Iron Man hit him hard. Then Iron Man turned and hit Barnes. Suddenly, Iron Man brought the walls down with his superpowers. Everything crashed down around them.

"Get out of here!" Captain America shouted to Barnes.

Barnes ran and Iron Man tried to stop him.

"It wasn't *him*, Tony! It was Hydra. They brainwashed him!" shouted Captain America.

Iron Man received a voice message from his secretary. "You're losing power," she told him.

Barnes tried to climb out of an open door in the roof, but Iron Man stopped him. He threw Barnes down on the floor.

"Do you even *remember* them?" he asked Barnes angrily.

"I remember *all* of them," Barnes replied.

"You can't change the past," Captain America said to Iron Man.

"That doesn't matter," said Iron Man. "He killed my mom."

KAPOW! WHAM! He attacked Rogers and Barnes again.

Iron Man turned to Captain America and asked angrily, *"Did you know?"*

Can They Forgive?

While Captain America and Iron Man fought inside, Zemo was sitting in the snow outside, thinking about his dead family. Black Panther arrived and put down his mask.

"I almost killed the wrong man," he said. Zemo turned. "This is what you wanted … You wanted to see them destroy themselves and their friends," Black Panther continued. "You wanted to avenge the deaths of the people that you loved."

"My father lived outside the city," Zemo said. "I thought he was safe there. I took my family to his house. My son loved super heroes. He was excited when he saw Iron Man from the car window. I told my wife, 'Don't worry. They are only fighting in the city. We are a long way away from there.' When the screaming stopped, I searched for two days for their bodies. My father was still holding my wife and my son in his arms. And the Avengers? They went home. I knew that I couldn't kill them. More powerful men than me have tried. But I *could* start a civil war between them. I wanted them to kill their friends." Then he said, "I am sorry about your father. He seemed a good man— with a good son."

"You have destroyed your own life with hate," said Black Panther.

"It is destroying them, too. It is not going to destroy me."

Zemo put his gun to his head, ready to kill himself. Black Panther pushed the gun away.

"The living have not finished with you yet," he said.

Inside, Iron Man continued attacking Captain America. Captain America's face was covered in blood, but he fought back.

"Bucky's my friend," said Captain America.

"*I* was your friend, too," said Iron Man. He hit him hard and Captain America fell again. "Stay down," he said.

Captain America got up very slowly. "I can do this all day," he said.

He pushed his shield into the power center on Iron Man's body suit. The power died; Iron Man couldn't fight now.

Then Captain America pulled the shield away, slowly walked over to Barnes, and helped him to his feet.

"That shield doesn't belong to you!" said Iron Man angrily. "My father made it!"

Rogers dropped the shield and walked away, holding Barnes up. Iron Man tried to get up, but fell back on the floor.

Some weeks later, Zemo was interviewed in prison by Everett Ross.

"After all that time, all that work, how does it feel to fail?" Ross asked.

"*Did* I fail?" Zemo replied, with a small smile.

Tony Stark went to the Avengers' main office building. Rhodes was learning to walk again. He was glad to see his friend.

They walked together very slowly. When Rhodes fell down, he refused Stark's help. He had to get stronger and do things for himself.

"I flew 138 times in wars against our enemies," he told Stark. "I flew because the fights needed to be fought. It's the same with the Sokovia Accords. I signed because it was right. I still believe that."

There was a knock on the door—a man with a package for Stark. It was from Rogers, and there was a letter:

Tony, I'm glad you're back in the office. All of us need family. The Avengers are yours. Maybe they're more yours than mine. I've been alone since I was eighteen. I never really fit in any group. I believe in people ... like those who became my friends. Most of those friends have always helped me. And that's why I have to help them, too. I know I hurt you, Tony. I didn't tell you about your parents because I didn't want you to suffer. But I can see now that I was really protecting myself. And I'm sorry. I hope that one day you'll understand. You're doing what you believe in. That's what all of us do. That's what is right. So if you need me, I'll be there.

There was a knock on the door—a man with a package for Stark. It was from Rogers, and there was a letter.

Activities

Chapters 1–2

Before you read

1   Look at the Word List at the back of the book. Check the meaning of new words and discuss these questions.

   a Which would most people like to meet, a *hero* or a *terrorist*? Why?
   b What do you know about *super heroes*? Do you have a favorite super hero?
   c In what way are a *mask* and a *shield* similar? What is the difference between them?

2   Look at the pictures on the Who's Who? pages at the front of the book. Which of these people do you know, from books and movies? Discuss what you know about them.

3   Now read the information in Who's Who? and answer the questions.

   a What have you learned about Captain America's shield?
   b Who was brainwashed by a terrorist organization?
   c Which Avenger is a robot?

4   Read the Introduction that follows Who's Who? Explain in your own words why, in this story, Avengers will fight Avengers.

While you read

5   Who:

   a destroyed Hydra? ....
   b brainwashed Barnes in Siberia? ....
   c became the Winter Soldier? ....
   d stole chemicals in Long Island? ....
   e kills Karpov in Cleveland? ....

6 Write the correct names.

a Captain America is in Lagos with Falcon, Scarlet Witch, and

....

b They are trying to stop an attack by ....

c He steals deadly .... but Black Widow takes them back.

d .... can't stop a fire destroying part of a hotel.

After you read

7 Discuss these questions.

a Why are these important to the story?
a small red book   bags of chemicals   Hydra   December 16, 1991

b What happened in these places?
Siberia   Cleveland   Lagos

c Are the Avengers successful in Lagos? Why (not)?

Chapter 3

Before you read

8 Read the Introduction to the book again. Why does Captain America not like the Sokovia Accords?

9 After the bombing in Lagos, will people think that the Avengers are still heroes? Why (not)?

While you read

10 Who is speaking?

a "The terrorists were criminals—but the Avengers were also working illegally."   ....

b "Sometimes we can't save everybody. We have to live with that."   ....

c "You don't seem to think about ordinary people's lives. Many get hurt."   ....

d "I don't think we should keep people awake at night in fear. We should sign."   ....

e "If we don't sign this now, they'll punish us later." ....

f "Everyone, get down!" ....

After you read

11 Work in pairs. Act out the conversation between Tony Stark and Steve Rogers after Secretary Ross leaves the room.

Student A: You are Tony Stark. Talk about your weapons, Charlie Spencer, and your reason for agreeing to sign the Sokovia Accords.

Student B: You are Steve Rogers. Why is it wrong for the Avengers to agree to the Accords? Explain.

12 Why are these people in, or not in, the United Nations building in Vienna when the bomb explodes?

a Natasha   **b** King T'Chaka   **c** Captain America

Chapter 4

Before you read

13 Discuss these questions.

a This chapter is called "The Search for Bucky Barnes." Who do you think will search for him? Why?

b Since the Sokovia Accords, what will happen to the Avengers if they continue to fight in other countries?

While you read

14 Circle the correct answers.

a Who wants to avenge his father's death?
Bucky Barnes   Steve Rogers   Prince T'Challa

b Who refuses to help Rogers find Barnes?
Sam Wilson   Natasha Romanoff   Sharon Carter

c Where does Captain America find Barnes?
a Bucharest, Romania   b New York, U.S.   c Vienna, Austria

d What is not made of a strong metal from Wakanda?
 Captain America's shield   Prince T'Challa's suit
 Falcon's wing suit
e Who says to the police, "Everyone stop! Don't shoot!"?
 War Machine   Bucky Barnes   Prince T'Challa
f Who orders Sharon Carter to take Rogers's, Wilson's, and Prince T'Challa's weapons?
 Thaddeus Ross   Everett Ross   Tony Stark
g Who has Stark put in a "safe place" with Vision?
 Natasha Romanoff   Sharon Carter   Wanda Maximoff
h What does Stark want Rogers to do?
 sign the Sokovia Accords   put Wanda in prison   look after Wanda

After you read

15 Which statements about Bucky Barnes do you know are true (✔)?

a He was Rogers's friend for many years. ◯
b He was brainwashed in Bucharest. ◯
c As the Winter Soldier, he is a killing machine. ◯
d He killed Prince T'Challa's father. ◯

16 What have you learned about these people in this chapter?

a Prince T'Challa   **b** Sharon Carter   **c** Wanda Maximoff

17 Who believes that Barnes bombed the United Nations building in Vienna? Why? Who doesn't believe it? Why?

18 Discuss why these people are in trouble. What will happen to them, do you think?

a Captain America, Falcon, and Black Panther
b Barnes

Chapter 5

Before you read

19 In Chapter 1, Zemo took the little red book from Karpov's apartment. What do you think he plans to do with it? Why?

While you read

20 Are these statements correct (✔) or incorrect (✘)?

    a Barnes was interviewed in the Berlin police station. ⬡

    b Someone wanted the Avengers to find Barnes, Rogers decides. He doesn't know why. ⬡

    c Barnes's interviewer is an American doctor. ⬡

    d Zemo organizes the bombing of a power station so he can kill Barnes. ⬡

21 Who is he? Write his name.

    a He killed Tony Stark's parents. ....

    b He will have power over all the Winter Soldiers. ....

    c He knows someone who can help Captain America. ....

After you read

22 Re-tell, in your own words, the story of what happened on December 16, 1991.

23 What have you learned in this chapter about:

    a Hydra's Winter Soldiers?   **b** Zemo?

Chapters 6–7

Before you read

24 Discuss these questions.

    a What do you know about Spider-Man?

    b How will Captain America find people with the right skills to join his team?

While you read

25 Circle the correct words to describe Spider-Man and his skills.

high school student   *prince*   *secret*   *shield*   *Avenger*
red and black suit   *wings*   *webbing*   *adult*   *climber*

26 Who is going to fight with Captain America (C.A.)? Who is going to help Iron Man (I.M.)? Who don't we yet know about (?)?

a Vision ....
b Hawkeye ....
c Scarlet Witch ....
d Spider-Man ....
e Falcon ....

f Ant-Man ....
g War Machine ....
h Black Panther ....
i Black Widow ....

After you read

27 Complete the sentences.

a Wanda attacks Vision so she can …
b Scott Lang wants to help …
c Captain America wants to find …
d Natasha doesn't want Avengers …
e She doesn't want a …

28 Work in two groups. One group is Captain America's team and the other is Iron Man's. Decide which super hero each of you is. Discuss what will happen if you fight a civil war. Is there any other way?

Chapters 8–9

Before you read

29 Discuss how the Avengers' civil war will be different from a civil war between ordinary people or soldiers.

While you read

30 Who is speaking? Write the name.

a "I don't want you to start a civil war." ....
b "Barnes is mine!" ....
c "I have to do a good job for Mr. Stark." ....
d "If some of us are going to win this fight, some of us are going to have to lose it." ....
e "Give me back my Rhodey!" ....

After you read

31 Discuss who on Iron Man's team helps Captain America. How?

Chapters 10–11

Before you read

32 Who or what will Captain America and Barnes find in Siberia, do you think? What will happen to Barnes?

While you read

33 Who feels that they have made a mistake? Circle the names.

Black Widow	*Vision*	*Scarlet Witch*
Iron Man	*Falcon*	*War Machine*
Zemo	*Captain America*	*Clint Barton*

34 What was Zemo's plan? Write Yes or No. He wanted:

a to avenge the deaths of his family. ....

b to become an Avenger. ....

c to kill Dr. Broussard so he could interview Barnes. ....

d to start a civil war between the Avengers. ....

e to make Captain America a Winter Soldier. ....

f Iron Man to kill Captain America. ....

After you read

35 Discuss these questions.

a Do you feel sorry for Stark, Barnes, or Zemo? Why?

b How have the Avengers' feelings for other Avengers changed by the end of the story?

Writing

36 Write a report for television news about the Sokovia Accords and the bombing of the United Nations Building in Vienna.

37 In what ways is the idea of Sokovia Accords a good one? What are the problems with the agreement? Do you think that super heroes should sign it?

38 The civil war has ended. Write a letter to Secretary of State Thaddeus Ross. Tell him what should happen to Barnes, in your opinion. Can Barnes be useful to him?

39 Write a report for the *Sokovia News* comparing the two Sokovians, Wanda Maximoff and Helmut Zemo. How did their lives change after the bombing in Sokovia? Who chose the best way to avenge the deaths of their family?

40 You are Iron Man. It is six months since you received Captain America's letter. Write a letter back to him. Tell him how you feel about him now.

41 Write ten questions that you would like to ask King T'Challa. Write his answers.

42 You have superpowers and you want to become an Avenger. Write a letter to Steve Rogers. Tell him about your superpowers. Explain why you want to join the team.

43 Write a plan for a short movie that follows *Captain America: Civil War*. Do they still work together? Who is the enemy now?

Word List

accords (n pl) agreements

avenge (v) to punish someone who has hurt you or other people

bomb (n, v) a *weapon* that can destroy people and buildings with a sudden loud noise

brainwash (v) to change someone's ideas or beliefs. Then they think in ways that you want them to think.

bullet (n) a small, metal thing shot from a gun

chemical (n) something that can be carefully mixed with others by scientists—for medicines or *weapons*, for example

civil war (n) a war between two groups of people who usually live in the same country

drone (n) a machine that flies through the air without a driver

explode (v) to break into many small pieces with a sudden loud noise. An *explosion* can kill people and destroy buildings.

helicopter (n) a vehicle that flies. Unlike an airplane, it can go straight up in the air and can land in a small area.

hero (n) someone who is very brave and popular

mask (n) something that covers your face, for protection

power (n) the ability to do something. A *powerful* person is very strong or important.

robot (n) a machine that can act like a person. Robots often look like people, too.

shield (n) something that you hold in front of your body. It protects you from attacks.

super(-) (adj) more, better, or bigger than usual

terrorist (n) a person who hurts other people unlawfully for political reasons. The criminal acts of a terrorist are *terrorism*.

weapon (n) something that you fight with, like a gun or a knife

webbing (n) a strong, natural material which is made by some small animals

wing (n) one of the two parts on a bird's body that make flying possible